RUNNING WITH WOLVES

by Megan Howard   illustrated by Joe Weissmann

Table of Contents

D1378197

Chapter 1
HOMEWORK TIME

Evan's mother walked into the living room.

She turned off the TV set.

"Time to stop watching TV," she told him. "You need to do your school work."

Evan had to write a report about wolves. But he wanted to sit with his older brother, Toby. "This show is about wolves," Evan told her.

"That's fiction. It's not real," his mother said. "You need to read some nonfiction books or magazines."

"I'm tired. I played soccer all day," he told her. "It was a tough game."

Soccer was Evan's passion. He loved the sport and he was a great player.

"And now it's time to do your homework," his mother said again.

Evan stood up and walked toward his bedroom. "It's not very exciting," he said.

His mother smiled warmly. "Maybe it will be more exciting than you think."

Chapter 2
A SURPRISE

Evan looked at the pile of library books on his desk. He grabbed one off the top and sat on his bed. He started to read. It was hard to concentrate.

Then Evan noticed a photograph. He saw a pack of wolves chasing a deer. "Wow!" he thought. He turned the page and saw a wolf pup. It was so cute.

Evan went back to the beginning of the book. He read every word.

Evan finished looking at the books. He wanted to know more. He turned on his computer.

But by now Evan was even more tired. "I'll just rest a little," he mumbled. He put his head down, and fell asleep.

Chapter 3
THE HUNT

When Evan woke up, his stomach ached. He was hungry.

Something else felt strange. Evan looked down. He was standing in the snow. Then he saw a pack of gray wolves near him. The wolves ignored him.

Evan looked down. He had become a wolf too!

He sniffed the air and smelled a buffalo. It was dinnertime. He knew that wolves could go two weeks between meals. But he was so hungry. He wanted food now.

He also knew that every pack has a male leader. No wolf seemed to be in charge. "Am I the leader?" Evan wondered.

"Aaaa-ooooo!" he howled. The pack came to him. That was it! He was the leader!

11

Evan ran through the snow. The others followed. As he ran he thought about what he had read.

He had to be careful. He could not lead the wolves into another pack's area. It was too dangerous.

Evan saw the buffalo ahead. Together the wolves formed a circle around it and tried to trap it. But the buffalo got away. Evan and the others were tired. They did not bother to run.

Evan felt bad. He knew that the leader ate first. But since they didn't have food, no wolf would eat.

All of a sudden, something pushed Evan. Was it another wolf who wanted to become a leader?

Then Evan heard Toby say, "I guess reading about wolves *was* boring."

Evan rubbed his eyes. "No way. Life can be hard for a wolf. I really admire them."

"Dinner is ready. You can tell me all about it while we eat," Toby said.

Evan couldn't wait to tell his brother about his splendid dream.

Comprehension Check

Summarize

Use a chart to tell about
events in the story.
Then use the chart to
summarize the story.

Alike	Different

Think and Compare

1. Reread pages 8–9. Which part of
   the text is real? Which part is not
   real? *(Compare and Contrast)*

2. Why is a fantasy story fun to read?
   (Synthesize)

3. There are wolves in some national
   parks. Some people think they should
   not be allowed to live there. Others
   disagree. What is your opinion?
   (Evaluate)